AF322589

Table of Contents

<u>New House</u>

"This new house will be great!"
They said "It has that vintage charm"
And although I have to live here now,
My fear, I can't disarm.

There's something about this house
I've seen a grim and taunting face,
I really wish we could pack our bags
And move far from this place

But my parents do not notice
The moving portraits on the walls
Nor the glowing eyes that leer
From the shadows in the halls.

When I say this house is haunted
They laugh and disagree
(But I really think this would explain
How we got this house for free)

<u>**Goblin's Feast**</u>

A piggish snout and sauerkraut

Went in the goblin's stew.

With a side of fries and reptile eyes

And ketchup that's turned blue.

As the smell of feet and questionable meat

Pass through the kitchen door,

The guests arrive with forks and knives

Demanding food galore

They scarf down ooze and purple goos

And slimy, grimy gunks.

They lick their bowls clean as their jowls turn green

And chomp on meaty chunks.

You would not be ready for their spaghetti

For it looks like worms and hair,

And yet they devour what grew from a shower

As a delicacy, they swear.

But in the bubbling,

Curdling, fermented stew

Some may wonder what it is they brew

but their secret ingredient

Are children like YOU!

Ancient of the Ocean

Within the dark ocean
Beyond the abyss
A creature there lurks
Where no light can kiss.

It's skin secretes mucus
That's putrid and foul
With suction cup arms
And a beak like an owl.

It preys on large sharks
And can grapple a whale
And feasts on poor sailors
Who above it set sail.

It has one single eye
To gaze far and wide
And no known harpoon
Can puncture its hide.

Beware it's cruel ink
That makes waters blacken
Beware this vile creature
Whose known as the Kraken.

<u>Wishing</u>

Many "wish upon a star"
While awake in bed they lay
ut how could anything hear you
From millions of miles away?

You can wish upon a droplet
Of glossy morning dew,
days are bad and nights are sour
To start each day anew.

You can wish upon a leaf,
ho shift with time and seasons,
ey understand the change of hearts
motives, rhymes and reasons.

If you were to wish upon a star,
It could be on the Sun we know
For there would be no life without his
rays
Beneath his mighty glow.

You could wish upon the moon
Who is a light when all is dark,
Or on a tree that gives us life
Making air from leaves and bark.

So why look beyond our sky
When there's so much here in surplus
There are wonders in the water,
In the forest, and the air
That can all be found around us.

<u>**Nyctophobia**</u>

There is an unease in the dark

I just can't comprehend.

It makes my stomach tingle

And makes my fear ascend.

My toys that bring me joy

Become menacing in the dark.

Their shadows twist and spiral

With faces grim and stark.

My parents took from me

My only way to cope

(Without my trusted night light

I've lost all sense of hope.)

As my fear grew greater,

I noticed morning's light

Banishing the night sky,

Relieving me of fright.

I may not be the bravest

(At least I'm not quite yet)

But I will always try to be

Each night the sun has set.

<u>Vampire Guy</u>

Gliding through the clear night sky

With leathery wings, I flap and fly.

As mortals flee from my deafening cry

For I am a fearful vampire guy.

From in my coffin, I creep and spy

Lurking in my tower high,

But cloves of garlic I will not buy,

For I am a terrifying vampire guy.

Dressed up in a suit and tie,

When in the sun, my flesh will fry!

And if you were to ask my "why"?

I am a horrible vampire guy.

If you cannot identify

Who I am, I'll clarify

For all my days, I'll testify

That I am a hungry vampire guy.

Sick Day

When I looked in the mirror
To fix my hair
I gave myself
The biggest scare

My skin had gone purple
With bright orange spots
And hair was all tangles
In large, matted knots

So I told my mother
That I should skip school
But she made me go anyways
Or I'd end up a fool.

My eyes started swelling
With lime green puss
My teacher then scolded
"Stop making a fuss!"

When I returned home
Covered in sores
My father demanded
I start on my chores

Does nobody see
How sick I look?
This disease can't be found
In any medical book.

A full night of rest
Is just what I need
But first I'll settle down
With a book to read.

Hallow's Eve

From out of the forest
I crept through the dark
And stumbled upon
A pumpkin lined park.

I expected to find
At least one human child
But these creatures instead
Were dazzling and wild.

Although I smelled children,
Not one could be seen
Instead I found zombies
And goblins all green.

I watched as they sauntered
And knocked door to door
Collecting sweet candies
In bags down to the floor.

I wondered what prompted
This grand cabaret?
And what made the humans
All move away?

It seems that these monsters
Are all here to stay
Here on this splendid
Hallow's Eve Day.

Painting

Today I started painting
On a canvas made of wood,
Making every brushstroke
As life-like as I could.

But then my art piece flickered,
And I swore the eyes did blink,
Her hair began to tousle,
And her cheeks turned rosy pink.

My creation looked around
And mirrored my every motion
Puzzled by her new limbs,
Herself and her emotions.

She looked around her picture frame
And placed her hand against my own
But I realized if I left her here
She would sadly be alone

I took my brush once more
In awe of what I created
And painted her a friend
So, she too would be elated.

<u>**Where Have All the Children Gone?**</u>

Where have all the children gone

Who pretended sticks were swords?

Who chased the fairies into the night?

Who drew out runes and wards?

Where are all the make-believers?

All the warriors and magic makers?

Who believed that rocks were dragon eggs?

Who were gourmet mud-pie bakers?

I see them through their windows

Glued to their moving screens

Wishing for adventure

Beyond their garden greens.

Why do all the children

Never leave their home?

Sitting in their rooms

No longer do they roam.

I miss the days of magic

I miss the hours of play

But from morning dawn

Until moonlight's rest

Within their homes they stay

<u>The City</u>

The city is far too noisy

With its sirens, cars and horns.

I'd rather prick my finger

On a bush of berry thorns.

I cannot stand the smell

Of smog and car exhaust.

I'd rather stand in snow

And be in cold and frost.

The people walk the streets

Without gazing at each other

Rushing through their days

As though each person's just a number.

When will they start to play?

When will they want to connect?

Though they live so close together

Their community they neglect.

<u>Lost</u>

Beyond the moon and milky way

Past meteor fields and mines

Above the edge of the celestial abyss

One saddened soul's hope declines.

Upon a drifting debris of star

Floating off in space

A single, dismal, distressful though

Brought sorrow to his face

"Perhaps I am

The last of my kind….

The last of the human race"

<u>Moving Day</u>

Beneath the leaves,

The twigs and soot

My house was crushed

By a mighty foot.

A human child

Now roams these lands

With long braided hair

And ten fingered hands

Her relentless stomping

Just won't do!

I'll pack my bags

And find somewhere new!

But where could I go?

A Leprechaun I?

I can't even swim

Nor can I fly!

Perhaps a journey

Is just what's needed

Before my patience

Is all depleted.

The Hunt

I feel its eyes upon me,

For soon the beast will pounce

Her golden eyes fixated

On her prey she plans to trounce.

I see her keen ears flatten

Once pointed up, astounding

Surveying every movement

In her lair and surrounding.

Her claws retract like razors,

Her teeth are sharpened too!

She takes a breath and bellows out

A high pitched, gentle "mew".

Her fur feels like cotton!

With this creature, I am smitten.

Although she may protest,

she's just the cutest kitten

<u>**The Werewolf Pup**</u>

In the depths of the forest

A werewolf took root

Whose sharp eyes gleamed silver

With a long, pointed snoot.

Although the fierce beast

Thought himself a cruel brute

All who beheld him

Found him quite cute.

His sharp teeth were knives

That could tear into bone

And he's pursue prey

In the darkness alone.

But all creatures were safe

From his hunts, he'd postpone

For he was too tiny

And not fully grown.

<u>**Into the Beast**</u>

Travelers gather to where I rest

In search of glory and gold.

With torches in hand

They all caravan

To what they think is a cave

(I have been told.)

But to keep from snoring

My mouth is agape

(Luckily for them,

Their only escape)

<h1 align="center"><u>Life in the Stars</u></h1>

Maybe I'm better suited

For life beyond the stars

The Earth is too congested

With buildings and with cars.

I might prefer the moon

(I've heard it's made of cheese)

But then I'd miss the ocean

And it's salty scented breeze.

I could make a home on Saturn

And picnic on it's rings.

Like when I'd hike through mountains

To find lovely hidden springs.

But it would be best to live on Pluto

So I'd be far and left alone

Where no one there could reach me,

Not by mail or by phone.

<u>Normal</u>

Have you ever wanted to be normal?

Oh how boring that would be.

I would rather be strange and silly

And mischievously carefree.

I would rather take a hidden path

Then take the same paved road

For dull and dreary monotony

Would make my mind erode.

I would rather tame a walrus

And help him climb a tree

Or even meet a Yeti

And give him a cup of tea.

For the world is filled with impossibles

And many who will tell you "No".

Instead, put on a smile

And make your life a show.

Monster in My Attic

There's a monster in my attic
And I don't know what to do!
He has eaten all of my pillows
And even my left shoe.

I've told him "Hey! Go Away!
Go back to where you're from"
But then he hopped up on my shoulder
And filled my hair with gum.

He behaves well when he's sleeping
Though his snoring keeps me awake
(He sounds much like a hippo
Gurgling deep beneath a lake.)

I trapped him in a cardboard box
And thought I stood a chance.
But when I locked him in my closet
He shredded all my pants.

Perhaps I should just move out
He's won this final round
It's just not worth this headache
And feeling like I'm bound.

So I packed my bags and headed
And moved to a new place
But what I found in my luggage.
Was an all too familiar face.

<u>**Attitude**</u>

If the world outside is bitter
And everyone seems rude
You can choose to mope or flitter
Or change your attitude.

You can try to be the kindness
You strive to see each day
While others live in blindness
And simply walk away.

For every effort that you make,
No matter who it's for,
Can help a hardened heart awake
To spread good will and more.

Although our world's not perfect
And people seem apart,
A genuine smile can brighten a day
And open a calloused heart.

The Meekest Voice

From the whisper of an ember's glow,

From a small seed can a great tree grow,

And the meekest voice, I hope you know

Can topple mountains high and low.

If every puddle from a rain's downpour

When gathered could be an ocean's roar

For the tallest wave, they can soar

from drops of water gathered more

When hope is gone and all seems dark

From just a thought, change can spark

to choose the roads we will embark

to humble those who yell and bark

<u>Beneath my Bed</u>

Perhaps there is no monster

To fear beneath my bed.

What if my closet's creaking

Was simply in my head?

I suppose those glowing eyes

Could be a trick of light

And not a horrid creature

Stalking me each night.

Hurray for a Boring Day

Today I was feeling bored

What an amazing way to feel

To be driven to do something else

Something creative, new and real

As I look around my house

I cannot help but wonder

What drove the herds to build their homes

To escape the snow, wind and thunder

I wander around a park

And hear a busker playing

I watch children reading books

About monsters and dragon slaying

How boring then, our own world would be

If our every whim was met

And look forward to all the realities

That have not been thought of yet

www.ingramcontent.com/pod-product-compliance
Lightning Source LLC
Chambersburg PA
CBHW020845150726

48196CB00002B/231